I0520891

Highlander Bride Taken

Omnibus Edition

By

Lynda Belle

Shadowcat Publishing

San Jose, California

Format: Omnibus Edition

Author: Lynda Belle

Cover Design:

Editor: Claudette Cruz

Beta Readers: Alain Gomez and Lisa Frogjourney

ISBN: 0-9978170-1-1
ISBN-13: 978-0-9978170-1-0

To all my friends that participate in Scottish Games and
The Northern California Renaissance Fair.
This is for our love for those men in kilts.

CONTENT

Highlander Bride Taken

Scottish Erotic Tales Book 1

Chapter 1

May 18, 1712

The castle loomed before me. My wedding was imminent. My fate was sealed as I moved closer to my future prison. I was to be a bridal tribute between my father and Lord McFarris to seal the clan truce. Peace would reign between the clans. I had to go through with it and become the new Lady McFarris or have the blood of my family spilled.

I didn't mind saving my clansmen from future fighting and bloodshed. The problem was that Lord McFarris was eighty-one years old, grey around the areas that counted the most for a man. My eighteen-year-old body would be new to the delights described to me awaiting in the wedding bed. Would he be able to excite me?

Oh, how I wish a younger man could take me. Something I'd dreamed for myself since the times my sisters gossiped after their wedding nights. The things they talked about. The touches their husbands did upon their bodies.

I hoped something like that would happen even if my new husband were a living corpse. I was resigned to my fate. Little did I know of the surprise that awaited me inside those stone walls.

The carriage eased up the embankment to the gates. The swaying of the carriage made me uneasy as the edge loomed next to me. Maybe it would be easier to topple over the side and end it all. Nothing to think about. No one to blame. A simple accident to end my torment of the uncertain. But then the peace wouldn't be upheld and my cousins could die in battle.

I leaned out of the window opening, clasping the edge looking down into the canyon below. The wind swept back my red hair, an indication of my fiery and passionate temper. A Scotswoman knew her duty. I couldn't falter. But if I opened the door, I'd tumble out. A mere accident of a troublesome latch. I shook off the temptation and returned back to the comfortable pillows lining the hard bench inside. I leaned into the welcomed comfort knowing I'd made my choice. Marriage over death.

—

We pulled into the courtyard. The wheels warbled as we made the transition from the gravel road to cobblestones. The household was out to welcome the new lady of the house. All were standing looking in my direction.

The carriage came to a stop and a man stepped forward from the group. He wore a kilt of the McFarris clan, white shirt, and had long, wavy, flowing hair. His jaw line and chest had angles that made my heart flutter and do flips. It got my hopes up that this was to be my Lord. I knew he was too young, but I dreamed that he might be.

I came forward as I opened the door to get out. He held forth his hand for me to take. The carriage wobbled as I stood on the step leading down to the packed dirt. I tumbled forward and he caught me. His strong hands clasped my waist as I grabbed his arms for support. I could feel the muscle tone of his arms. The hair beneath my fingertips made me want to caress his arm. I wanted to feel the strength within those arms around me. God, if this were my lord, I would happily be taken tonight as a new bride.

He helped me to steady before taking my hand to meet the people gathered in the courtyard. The others assembled wore the McFarris kilt. Among them a woman looked sternly at me, sizing me up. I know they saw my petite figure, long red tresses curling unruly before them. I was being sized up for my birthing strength. My job was to make a new lord for the household. Did I have the figure to pull it off?

But the men were looking at me differently. I stepped forward to approving nods.

He led me to stand before the people gathered in the courtyard. "Good morrow, my lady. This is my clan. They stand before you in welcome to claim you as an addition to our family." The young man still held my hand as if I would break.

"Thank you for welcoming me. I stand before you a tribute bride for the peace and wellbeing of both our clans." I tried to speak with the dignity my heritage gave me. I was representing my people. I knew my father and mother would be proud. Today I was to become a woman.

"Your brothers have already arrived to be witnesses for the marriage. The ladies are ready to prepare you for tonight's ceremony." He let go of my hand. I felt the cold reach my fingers where his strong hand had made warm.

"Thank you, my lord."

"You may call me Lord McFarris." My heart skipped at the mention of his name. Could it be? Was he to be my lord for tonight's ceremony?

His next words sunk my heart. "My uncle is too fragile today to greet you. He can't make it down to see you. He has sent me in his stead to welcome you. I am his nephew."

"Thank you, my lord." Hope sank as I realized my future nephew-in-law was standing before me. If only he was to be my Lord McFarris. But the words of my brothers rang true. Somewhere within the castle was the lord I was to marry, old and feeble, and I was to be his bride.

"Come, my lady, we shall prepare you for the festivities." A woman stepped forward, a smile on her face. She was plump and motherly, as tender as my own mother. "I am his lordship's sister. I will help you prepare for your bridal night."

I walked towards her only looking back for a moment to say, "Thank you for the heartfelt welcome, my Lord McFarris. I look forward to making this my home."

"I look forward to having you here, my lady." His smile lit up his face, his chiseled jaw lighting a fire within me.

My heart ached with a longing I'd not felt before now. I wanted him to take me tonight. My consciousness knew it would be wrong. But my future husband's nephew made my desire flare to new levels. A wedding night would be unforgettable with him. But if found, what would his cousins and my brothers do to us?

As I walked away, I could feel his eyes follow me as I entered the corridor into the castle.

Chapter 2

The feast after the ceremony was extravagant. I don't remember much about the ceremony except agreeing to marry the elder Lord McFarris. He was a bent-over wreck of a man, but well loved by his clan. He must have been much like his nephew in his prime. Now, he was skinny, grey hair rested upon his head and down his back. He wore the clan kilt proudly. He must have been a fine warrior. He glanced at me and smiled. I nodded and smiled back. I imagined the time with him tonight. His lips upon me. I'd feel like my grandfather was fondling me.

I turned to drink my wine and nudged his nephew's hand sitting next to me. His face had just a bit of new beard growth that I wished to touch. His smile made me want to know his lips upon mine.

He looked at me as if he would feast upon my large bosoms that pushed against my marriage dress, offerings for the lord that would conquer my womanhood this night. I was to be the sacrifice to the lord of the house to seal the clans as one.

I licked my lips after drinking some more of the wine. If only it was the nephew and not the uncle that would have me.

My new husband was nodding off in his chair, so I turned to my new nephew-in-law. He was devouring me with his eyes, his hand wrapped around his beer mug. "I am glad that the McPhersons sent my uncle such a beautiful bride. The lads that will be made will suit both clans."

"Yes. I do wish to be the vestal of much prosperity for both."

"Do you think you are fertile, my lady?"

"What kind of question is that, my lord?" I was a bit surprised by his forward question.

"It is my duty to make sure that the clan has an heir, my lady. I cannot marry until I am lord of the house. That cannot happen until my uncle passes to heaven. And I love my uncle. He lost all his sons in battle. He has treated me as his own son. I will treat his sons as my own."

He drank from his mug again. "I will not cause him harm, but I need to be assured that our clan will continue strong as ever." He lowered his glass and gently swept over my other hand. I didn't move it away, but met his glance. "I again ask, are you fertile, my lady?"

This time I did not falter. "Yes, my lord. I will bring your house many heirs. If there is enough left in my groom to take me tonight."

A sparkle lit his eyes. "Do not fear, my lady. You will be taken tonight. I guarantee it."

He took a long draught of the beer in his mug and stood at the table. He banged the mug down several times to get everyone's attention. The talking stopped. Everyone turned to listen.

"Everyone, thank you for coming to celebrate the joining of Clan McFarris and Clan McPherson. It is times like this that I am truly glad to celebrate peace and good tidings. For joining our clans will benefit many generations to come. And the generations will be started tonight."

The banging of mugs on the table resounded in an echoing throughout the hall. My nephew-in-law continued, "Tonight, my uncle will bed his new wife, and we will have a new heir strong in McFarris and McPherson blood. Long live the clans!"

Again, the banging of mugs answered my nephew-in-law. "Tonight, we celebrate the peace and prosperity that will be inherent in any marriage. Long live Lord and Lady McFarris!" He raised his mug to the resounding cry from all at the feast echoing his good faith in my marriage. "Long live Lord and Lady McFarris!"

After everyone had drunk to our good health, my nephew-in-law finished with, "Drink up, my lads, there is enough beer to fill the river below. But for my part, I could drink it all. Instead I've decided to share it with my closest friends and cousins. Let's celebrate until dawn."

With the last words, a cheer went up in the great hall, and the musicians took up a tune. He turned to me and offered his hand. "My uncle is too old to take you out for a proper bridal dance. I will do so in his honor. May I?" He offered his hand to me.

I didn't need to look over at his sleeping uncle. I took his hand in an instant, happy to be again in his strong arms.

He took me off the main table dais, and to the front of the hall. There, we welcomed the enchantment of the evening to take hold of our bodies as we started to form a circle for a dance. Others joined us, and I lost myself in the steps. The younger Lord McFarris would gaze at me across the other dancers. When our hands met during the dance, his touch sent shivers through my body that ached for more contact than a mere touch. I wanted more from him. I couldn't hide my blushes.

The dance ended, and we returned to the dais, as others continued to dance to the music. He helped me to sit and then whispered in my ear as he drew the chair back, "Tonight, I am to be your lord. Please, wait for me." He replaced the chair and I sat. He returned to his seat and looked at me, his hand stroking his chin.

His statement startled me. But I regained my composure and smiled. Maybe there was more to my fate than I knew. "My Lord, I do not know you first name as yet." The blush was starting again in the hopes he was to hold true to his word. "What may I call you besides nephew or my lord?"

"You may call me beloved."

Chapter 3

The women of the household took me not long after my beloved's statement. There was much anticipation from them. They wanted to dress me for my wedding night, and instruct me in all things a woman needed to know. The kind-looking woman that first introduced herself was indeed my sister-in-law, aunt to the younger Lord McFarris. She spoke to me gently as she undressed me out of my clothing in exchange for a nightdress. "A man likes his woman to look simple and vulnerable. You must let him do what he wishes. He is your lord now."

She pulled the heavy underskirts over my head, and left me with my nightshirt. Another lady of the house undid my hair, brushing it out so all the long, red curls shone in the candlelight. The older Auntie continued, "First, he may seem rough, but as you let him have his way, you will enjoy his attentions." She smiled a gentle smile as if she told other young girls these same words on their wedding night.

"You remind me of my gentle Sarah. Had she lived, she would have been your age now." The sorrow didn't last long. She clapped her hands and ushered the other women out of the room. One of the women left a pitcher and clay cup by the bedside. "Do drink some of the wine by the bedside, child. It will make things easier on you to be relaxed."

I went to the sideboard and poured a glass. By now the women had gathered my undergarments and were making their way out of the room. They sprinkled herbs and rose petals upon the bed to bless the union and wish fertility in the marriage. I knew the ritual. I had done it for my older sisters. It was now my turn to lie upon them and beget heirs for the clan.

Before she left, the kind Auntie turned to me. "Wait for him upon the bed. If he wishes anything else, he will let you know." And with that, she closed the door. I had nothing else to do but wait and drink the wine.

I walked about getting a sense of my new lord. The master bedroom had great furs covering the walls displaying the many beasts that had been killed on the hunt. Masculine prowess abounded in those displays.

I lay upon the bed feeling the soft straw stuffed within the mattress. I climbed inside the blankets to await my lord. The herbs created a mystical sweet scent of rosemary and lavender, easing my mind. The wine lulled me into an almost sleep. That is until the door opened.

In walked the elder Lord McFarris. He was still dressed in his wedding attire, head to foot the regal lord of the manor. But his stunted walk, complete with a cane, belied his virile dress. "Tis' time, my pretty."

I swallowed. "Yes, my lord." I leaned back in the pillows as he took up the other side of the bed. He grabbed at my red tresses that the woman had fanned out around me.

"Such a beautiful bride. Yes, indeed. The McPherson clan doth honor me well."

He climbed upon the bed, leaving his cane to clatter on the floor. Lying next to me, I could smell his putrid breath. The old always had that smell. I kept my honor, as I didn't flinch away from my new husband.

"Yes, quite pretty." He seemed to enjoy staring at me. So much so, he began to ease himself in the pillows next to me, and nudge me softly. He brought a hand to caress my cheek.

I looked into his eyes. They were the same as his nephew's. Suddenly, I thought of the younger Lord McFarris, and started to pretend it was him.

"So beautiful." He continued to look at me, caressing my cheek.

I clasped his hand and answered, "Yes, I am all yours." This brought a chuckle, almost an ecstatic burp from him. And his smile began to ease as he closed his eyes. He laid back into his pillow still smiling. He replied, "All mine." His breathing slowed, and I started to hear a snore escape his lips. My newlywed husband had fallen asleep.

The snores echoed in the chamber. I looked at him for a while to see if he'd wake up. He didn't. Slowly, I knew not what to do but to rise slowly out of the bed and pour some more wine. There was always the chance that my new husband would wake up with the need to consummate our marriage. I needed to be relaxed and ready if he did.

That's when I heard a knock at the door. I turned holding the pitcher and cup in hand. In walked the younger Lord McFarris. A small gasp left my lips before I could stop it.

He put his finger to his lips. "Do not fear, my lady. I was coming to check on my uncle's progress."

I blushed, not knowing what to do. I pulled up some of the blanket I'd wrapped around my shoulders from the chair. He came towards me and held my shoulders. "Do not be afraid. I expected as much from my uncle. I knew he was too old to consummate the marriage. Luckily, most have gone to sleep. No one will ever know what McFarris seed created the new heir."

Hope sprung in my heart once more. I let the blanket fall as he pulled me towards him. His lips reached mine, pulling them into his mouth. Shocks reached my inner regions. I didn't know such feelings existed until my beloved kissed me. "Come. My room adjoins my uncle's." He took me through another door I hadn't noticed.

Once in the room, he closed the door, locking us within. My wish had been fulfilled. I felt relief. I was to be his after all.

He pulled down the shoulder of my nightdress, and kissed down my shoulder. Shivers traveled down my spine as he pulled my hair back to kiss my neck. "I am so glad it's you." The words left my mouth before I could stop them.

He stopped his tender attentions for a moment. "Why?"

"Because I was hoping you were my Lord McFarris the moment you lifted me from the carriage."

These words were like a catapult for our actions. He took to my neck like a man without air. He breathed in my scent as I leaned against the wall, him pulling my nightdress downward. I let him do what he liked. I was happy to let the younger man take his uncle's place.

He freed me of my nightdress, letting it drop to the floor. My breasts pressed against him. His chest eased against me. "I've wanted you since you first arrived." He pulled me to him, nuzzling my hair; he whispered in my ear, "You've been driving me mad since your arrival."

He kissed me deeply. I returned as much as I could, pulling his lips into my mouth as he'd done. Then, I grew bold and started to draw away his shirt. I had the intense need to see what lay beneath it. I'd never explored a man's body before. I wanted suddenly to learn his.

He froze, letting me caress his neck and shoulders. I could feel the hardness of his physique. The swordplay of a warrior of any clan would build the muscles in his neck and shoulders to their peak. I hungered to feel more of him. I felt the front of his chest, caressing under his pecs, and admiring the shape of them from under the shirt. I felt for his nipples, and circled them with my fingers.

It seemed to put him over his limit. He gathered me up in his arms. My naked breasts pushed up against him. My hands felt him carry my rump as he lowered me to his bed. There were no herbs upon the mattress here. But this was my place to meet my fate on my wedding night. This was to be my delivery from the prison I'd imagined.

I lay naked before him. He took me in as a sight not seen by a starving man. He hungered in his eyes as he lay next to me, stroking my side, easing up to my breasts and then to my face. He turned onto his side and looked me in the eyes. "It is your first time, my love. It may hurt a bit. But I will be gentle."

I licked my lips and nodded. "I understand. Please take me gently, beloved." With this blessing on my part, he rolled on top of me. His shirt hanging out of his pants, he mounted me as a stallion only could.

He removed his shirt and tossed it aside. Then, he undid the buckle underneath his kilt. I watched, trying to not show the fear on my face. I wanted him, but I didn't want to be hurt.

He eased to the side of the bed to remove his kilt. Unwrapping it carefully, he placed it to hang on a chair. He stood before me. I saw the glory of a naked man for the first time. He was strapping as only a good Scotsman could be. His large chest showed the muscles well exercised and legs toned. He had hair upon his chest accenting the shapes of his pecs. I wanted to touch him, but I was unsure of the ways of the marriage bed. I had much still to learn.

He repositioned himself over me, and started to kiss me as he brought his body over me. I'd never known the feeling of being cradled by a man's body this way. His gentle pressure atop me felt reassuring and gentle. He leaned on me, kissing my neck, down my side, and to my navel. Then, he proceeded to an area I'd not known before. He moved down to my mid-thighs, and kissed each one. He lifted his head and parted my legs. "Do you trust me?"

I nodded. "Yes. I trust you."

"Good." His voice held amusement. Then, I found out why. He placed his tongue upon my womanly parts, and suckled like a pig finding substance. Suddenly, I knew why he had smiled. The sensation of passion drove through my body like lightning.

Each suckle brought new levels of ecstasy I'd not imagined. The more he licked and pulled, I thought nothing else could be like this until I felt the release of all he'd built. All thought escaped me as my passion exploded in my very being. I panted and moaned like I'd never before.

He climbed back atop me, leaned down and whispered, "That is what a woman can feel with her man every time if done correctly. Are you ready for more?"

"Aye, my lord. I am yours to take." I breathed deeply as he proceeded to take me further into the ways of marriage. I did wonder, what more could he do? Wasn't this the grandest thing a woman could feel? I was wrong.

He began to use his finger in mysterious ways upon my private person, stroking and moving the wetness that flowed over my inner region. Poking his finger inwards created sensations that made me arch my back.

He stroked me, again and again plunging inwards. My eyes closed as my moans took over a life of their own. Finally, I felt the overpowering release that freed me into shudders of passion. My lord had my body under his control, and I responded to his touch.

"Please my lord, what power is this you find within me?"

He chuckled and whispered to me as he mounted over my squirming body, "Tis' nothing more than a man pleasing his lady. I have experience in the ways of a woman's body, as such I wish to share over and over with you."

With this promise, he lowered his body onto me. His chest hair pressed against me as he grabbed my mouth in an embrace with his lips. I gave myself to him. His attentions were making me enslaved to his love. My mind forgot any fear of this prearranged encounter. I was becoming a woman.

He eased his groin down to me, rubbing his fingers over my inner parts to meet his head entering me. Slowly, I felt a pressure push inside me as my lord kissed me over and over. Then, he began to lean back, and mount me as the bride to be taken.

And then I felt the pain. For a moment it shot up my legs, and then the soreness started to abate. My intake of breath told him the pain had been caused with great gentleness. The look on his face was nothing but concern.

"It hurts not, my lord. I am a woman and bride this day. Please don't stop." I looked him in the eyes, and he glided back in again and again. This time the soreness started to end, and I began to feel his large size at the entrance of my maidenhood.

He began to mount me again, and push himself in and out at such a speed, the pleasure built in me again. I leaned back to receive his full length into my being.

Faster and faster he built my pleasure until I couldn't stop my release. The shudders shook me and then began in him. All thought was lost as my lord filled me with the seed of the McFarris clan.

It was done. I was a woman. He lay down next to me, holding me close as the soreness ebbed between my legs. The wind of the highlands blew outside the walls. It was a comforting sound to listen to while in the arms of my Scottish lord. And then I thought, all I know of him is that he is my beloved. I wanted to know his name.

"My lord, what may I call you besides beloved?" I paused before whispering, "What is your true name?"

He sighed, twisting a bit of my locks in his hand. "You may call me Conall."

Highlander Bride Seduction

Scottish Erotic Tales Book 2

Chapter 1

May 19, 1712

I heard the sounds of the early dawn as I lay in the arms of the man I loved. Bird song entered the window from the courtyard. I knew it would not be to our best interest to be found the day after my wedding in his bed. Conall was my nephew-in-law. I needed to return to my new husband's room through the connecting secret door. His uncle had been the groom the night before. But I wanted to stay in Conall McFarris's arms forever.

I snuggled up next to his neck, his long, wavy brown hair framing his face like a mane on a stallion. His angular face and morning stubble made me want to be taken again by him. He'd made me a woman instead of his eighty-one-year- old uncle.

I guess that made me a harlot. Or at least an adulteress. But if my husband hadn't fallen asleep, would he have taken me like Conall? I would never know the answer. I snuggled closer to Conall thinking maybe there was a way to make my husband think he did.

"Conall. Conall?"

He mumbled under his breath. Stirring slowly, he opened his eyes. His face broke with a smile when he saw me. "My dearest." He reached to kiss me, and I returned the passion, leaning across his chest to savor the feel of him.

"My love, I must return to my husband's bed. I do not want to think what would happen if I'm found in yours."

He nodded. "I knew you were a smart lass. You are right. You must return to his side." He gave me one last lingering kiss, and then swatted my bum. "Now, get with you. Though my uncle sleeps late, the rest of the household will want to check on his progress."

"What should I say?"

"Say what any lass says after her wedding night. You enjoyed it." He winked at me, and I toppled onto him again, dragging another kiss from his lips.

"Aye, I did my lord."

He swatted me again. "Now get to his bed. My uncle sleeps deeply. If you reenter quietly, I'm sure he'll hardly stir."

I got up to find my nightdress from the night before. I gathered it up and redressed. I went to the door as he whispered to me one last time. "Be sure to leave some drops of blood on your nightdress. The women will check."

I nodded as I slipped through the joining door. The bird song began to increase as I looked around for my husband's ceremonial dagger. Finding it hanging on a chair, I drew it from the scabbard. I took the point to my finger, and turned to add some droplets to the back of my nightdress. Sliding next to my still snoring husband, I waited under the thick blankets for the house to awaken.

I must have dozed off again. The women entering the bedchamber awoke me. Their chatter and excitement woke my husband. "Blessed day, my lady. We've come to check on your lordship and his lady." My new Auntie beamed with a joyful expression as she came to my side of the bed. "And we've come to dress you for your first day as Lady McFarris."

My elderly husband turned in his sleep as they ushered me through a door on the other side of the room. They started to undress me, taking the nightshirt eagerly to look for a sign of our consummation. Squeals of delight echoed in the room when they noticed the blood. The kind Auntie turned to me and said, "Indeed, you are a wife this day. Well met. There is much to do. You must meet the whole household. Not as a bride, but as the lady of the house now."

As they dressed me I wondered, how am I to hide this secret? How was I to be the wife of a lord I did not love? But the lover of his nephew that I did. I held back tears as they put me in one of the finest gowns I'd ever seen. Green velvet highlighted my red tresses as they fit me into my overdress. Pearls and garnet beads adorned the overdress and matching snood. The billowing sleeves wrapped about my arms. Green velvet slippers made me fit the appearance as the head lady of this noble house.

"The new lady must be at her best to be shown off to everyone. Today, you take your rightful place running the household. In several months, I'm sure you'll be a mother too." The cries of agreement made the women elbow each other in knowing acknowledgment.

I nodded to their attentions. If anything, I would do my duty in bringing the clans an heir. I would just have to hide the secret about how it was done. I wondered on this first day in my new home just how long it would be until I was with him again.

***

The next time I saw him, I was walking through the hall on my first inspection of the household. My new group of ladies-in-waiting surrounded me. Many of them had prepared me for my wedding night. They stood around me as a new guard assembled to keep men at a distance. He walked by nodding to me, and I tried to hide the blush.

"Good morrow, my lady." He took a moment to bow.

The other ladies halted. I took this as a cue that I should talk to him. "Good morrow." Words remained unsaid that pounded in my heart. I tried to stand up straight, and be the lady my mother had bred. "It is good to see you after such a long..." I paused for the word. "...Festive night." I was hoping my ladies didn't notice my hesitation on what to say. "Did everyone enjoy themselves?"

He stood at rest, his hands at his hips with a smile of amusement. "Yes, my lady. I think they did finish the ale, and then drank up the river below." The other ladies laughed, as did I. Some looked him over as the fine Scottish Lord he would make any woman. I wanted him to be mine.

I quickly answered, "Good to hear that everyone drank well. Did you enjoy the feast, my lord?"

"Yes. Very satisfying evening." He paused to smile at me. "I am glad my uncle has made such a wondrous match." His voice let nothing escape. His stature gave nothing away about last night. I was feeling that maybe it was to be our only time together.

The distant approach of his greeting was sending my heart into a panic. "I have duties I must attend to. My ladies are showing me my new domain. If you may excuse me, I'll be off to my womanly duties."

"As a woman should. Until we meet next time. I bid adieu."

Chapter 2

A castle is a small mini kingdom.
Everyone has the ears of an elephant. I know
why he was being careful. But it melted my heart
to see him again and again for a week without
much more than a glance or polite bow. Seeing
him fully dressed, his strong chest covered by
his tartan and shirt made me want to remove it. I
wanted to caress his firm chest, feel the soft hair
under my fingertips, and explore his body
further.

My lust had been unleashed. I wanted to
claim him as mine. But from the looks of my
ladies about me, they had sights on him. I would
learn later that it could have been my downfall.
It was wise to be secretive and not pursue until
there was the right moment. Stolen glances at
him while at dinner could be no more than
fitting in with my new family. After all, it is a big
change for any new bride to have to fit in with
her new clan.

I was the household female figurehead
now. At eighteen, I'd been bred for this kind of a

match. I felt ready to have a household of my own. My sisters had already been married off before me. It was my time.

The new life arranged for me was to keep my clan and the Clan McFarris allied for generations to come. I was to create the new generation within me. But I wasn't sure if one night with my young Lord McFarris would do the charm of making me with child.

I would settle into my bed at night, and sleep next to the elder Lord McFarris. He would fall asleep assuming he was the one that had taken me when he woke up. His age and his drink worked for me to cover the memory of the night before. I had not denied the assumptions everyone made. It made my grandfatherly husband seem more virile and in control again. My lord husband was helpful at dinner, instructing me in the way the manor was run. When he was forgetful, Conall would fill in.

One night after dinner, Conall sat with us as others rested about the hall. A visiting minstrel was strumming tunes on his mandolin. Ladies worked on the needlepoint and repairs needed for any castle. I worked on suitable embroidery for my lord husband's new doublet. It seemed that after my wedding, the household was returning to a regular schedule. Like the ebb and flow of the tides, life returned to a steady pace within the walls, accepting me as the new caretaker.

My lord husband began to nod in his chair, and I walked over to attend him. I placed a blanket over his legs to keep him warm. Returning to my needlework by the fire, I sat alone to be close to its warmth. Conall got up and came closer, taking a seat next to me by the hearth. Not a fortnight had passed since our night together. My heart fluttered with the anticipation.

"You are so kind to my uncle, my lady."

"It is a wife's duty to take care of her husband." I settled in my chair and took to my stitching with renewed care. I was hoping he didn't see the slight shake of my needle.

He leaned forward, holding his mug of ale. After drinking, he asked, "Are you feeling more at home now?"

"Yes, my lord. Everyone has been treating me with utmost care. I am quite pleased with the attentions of all my ladies. I did wonder about you, however?"

"Me? What have you wondered about?"

I looked up from my sewing to see him staring. My words had gotten his full attention. "If you were wondering how I was doing. Sometimes words are not enough. Sometimes I wish company too."

"Are you lonely?"

I looked at him and whispered, "Lonely and lost without you."

He drank again from his mug. Looking into the fire he said, "As am I."

My heart skipped when he said it. Did he long for me as much in the early morning hours? The longing for his caresses were keeping me up to all hours waiting to see if the door between our rooms would open again. Having tried recently, I'd found it locked. I didn't want to speak of these things as we were in the great hall. What was I to do without him?

He solved my dilemma by his next words. "Tonight, the door will be unlocked."

Chapter 3

I was standing in my nightgown in front of the connecting secret door between our bedchambers. Did I have the nerve to open it? My wedding night could be just a slip. A simple need to create an heir. But this. Knowingly going to him. It would be real adultery. I could be killed by any male of his kin or my own if they knew what we did.

I hesitated only for a moment. I longed to smell the scent of his body. I wanted to know what it would be like to have him within me again with no pain. My virginity had been taken and given to him freely. Could I give him my love now?

I tried the door. I heard the latch unlock. Pushing it open, I heard the breathing of my lord in his bed. I closed the door behind me, and let my nightdress fall to the floor. Moonlight spilled through the window slit in the wall. I could feel the floor rug beneath my bare feet. I walked toward the bed, taking time to watch my Lord Conall sleeping. I lifted the blankets and slipped in beside him. I shouldn't have.

He immediately woke up, grabbing me. Pulling a dagger from a secretive place, he held it to my neck. I didn't scream. I didn't breathe. I let him hold me until his eyes adjusted to the moonlight. I felt his hand relax and the dagger lower as he said, "My lady. Oh my god, my beloved. You awoke me." He held me by my shoulders, letting me unfold from his rough handling. "I knew not who you were."

He put the dagger under his pillow and wrapped his arms around me. He pulled me closer, stroking my hair. "I am so sorry. You must be careful when I'm alone. Any Scottish lord sleeps with his dagger in case someone tries to kill him in the night."

He kissed my head and pulled me onto his chest. He wore nothing beneath the blankets. I rested my head on his chest, stroking it. I was happy. I was with my lord. My naked body pressed up next to his. I slipped my body to fit his curves.

I had longed to be with him so much. I sighed as I lay on his chest, feeling that if anyone walked in on us, I'd happily die in his arms. Both my brothers and his cousins would kill us for being together. All I knew was this was where I wanted to be.

"We could die if we continue, my lord." I whispered the truth. To utter it was not making it any less dangerous.

He wrapped his arms around my back, and I nestled more to his side. "Aye. We could."

"I can't be without you. It has been more than a week. I can't stand to be without you any longer."

My words caused him to come alive in my arms. He turned to meet my body and kissed me. Each press of our lips together was nectar for our souls. My legs intertwined with his. Our bodies slipped together, locking us into an embrace. I could feel the movement of his hands up and down my body. I held him in my arms, his broad shoulders covering me as he took a position on top. He could crush me with his body, and I'd be content.

He kissed my eyelids. He traveled the course down my neck, stopping only to glide his lips down my skin. He caressed my shoulders and kissed them over and over until he slid down to my breasts. He stroked the pale skin, memorizing the curves of them with his fingertips. Then he grabbed the tip of one in his mouth, pulling on the nipple in such a fashion he built me towards the road of passion from my wedding night.

He sat up, cupping a breast with a twinkle in his eye. "What would you do if we were discovered now?"

"I'd want you to take me quickly, so I'd die with you inside me, beloved."

He lowered his lips to my ear. "I would happily die inside you."

I felt his fingers travel down the side of my body to end between my legs. I parted to let my lord have his way with me. I was completely his for evermore. He stroked my womanly parts into a wet frenzy. Pushing in and out with his fingers, he made the wetness spread to all parts of my womanhood. "Please my lord, take me as before. I will die if you don't."

He sat up, the stallion all ready to take me again. He took his man's head to explore the outside of my woman's opening. The sensations were building me up to receive the full length of his shaft. I was near begging when I said, "Please, Conall. I want you deep inside me. Let them find us locked together."

He plunged within. This time there was no pain, but the delicious thrilling rush of a man's shaft sliding along the entrance to my womanhood. Over and over again, he pushed inside me, until we could take it no more. I grabbed towards him, pulling him to go as deep as he could until he released all he had to give me.

The seed of the McFarris clan claimed me once again. An heir would be certain now. My husband could be easily convinced his prowess in bed was still intact if he had trouble remembering each night. I could fill in the blanks with compliments.

He lowered himself onto me as I wrapped my arms around him. I could feel him still inside me, and I didn't want to lose the feel of our union. Our breathing slowed, and he gently rolled off me. The blankets had rolled off to the sides of the bed, leaving us naked and exposed. I cuddled up next to him for warmth now that he was not atop me.

"How long can this go on, beloved?" His voice was gentle, exploring.

"I consider you my lord, Conall. Your uncle is my duty. But I love you." I searched for his eyes in the darkened room. I could feel his breath as his nose met the tip of mine.

"Aye. This could be a dangerous business, my love."

"Not if we tell no one. Your uncle does not really touch me except as a pretty token. He does not remember much from his drink. There needs to be an heir. It is our duty to do so."

"I think so too, my love. I thought my uncle might not do his duty on the night he married. I have been cautious in my endearment." He reached for my face, stroking my hair and down my cheek. "But we must make it all appear as if he has won your affections."

I grabbed his hand. I kissed the palm and let him caress my face. "I can act like he has pleasured me, and convince him he has made me a happy wife."

He stopped in mid-stroke. "I did not think you would take my heart as well. It was duty from the start. Now, it is more."

He began to kiss me again. Our passion was gentler, less desperate. We had some peace of heart at last. No matter what happened, we had this moment. We kissed as one being, stroking and exploring each other as newly discovered lovers.

I wanted to know every inch of his Scottish body. I caressed down his back and buttocks. I traveled down around the curve of his bum to his legs. He stopped kissing, letting me explore him. Hair accentuated his masculine definition. Long, flowing brown locks framed his face and down his back. He lay back, letting me take in his hard, masculine form. I was a newly made woman taken by the beauty of my lord's body.

Suddenly, I felt the urge to please him. I took my explorations downward, tracing one finger down to between his legs. He shuddered for a moment as I traced the top of his manhood. Skin covered the top, and I grew curious of what would happen if I pulled it downward. I wrapped my hand around his shaft. I stroked it, up and down, as he started to respond with a quiet moan from my attentions.

"I want to please you, my lord. What do you wish of me?"

There was only a moment. "Take me into your mouth. Please be gentle. Form your mouth into a circle." He put his hand behind his head. "It would please me the most."

"As you wish." I wet my lips. I leaned down and kissed the top of his manhood. He shuddered. Then, I turned the kiss into a suctioned kiss around the top of his shaft. My tongue worked in my mouth to taste him, forming circles around the tip. And then I wrapped my lips again, and took more of him into my mouth. I could not fit his full length, but for what I did hold I formed a perfect circle around him, moving up and down.

He began to squirm from my ministrations, which pleased me. I knew I was giving pleasure to my lord. I kept the pressure up and increased the speed of my actions until he let loose into my mouth the seed of the McFarris clan. This would produce no heirs. It left a salty taste in my mouth from his product.

Feeling my inner regions stir from pleasing my lord, I thought of the idea to mount my lord as he mounted me. The wetness helped me angle him as I slid up and down his shaft. He stirred again. This had been a lot of work for me to expect from a man. But I wanted him inside me again, and he began to grow hard with his need.

"My lord, shall we make sure there is an heir?"

"Aye, lass. It is your turn to take me."

I smiled as I angled his head to my opening. He moved his hips to help push into me as I kneeled over him. I came down on him as his shaft slipped into me as the perfect fit. I bent down upon him like a cat in heat, moving up and down as he pushed into my womanhood with the same rhythm. I found I could angle so his shaft fit over perfectly to build feelings within me to rise to new levels of pleasure.

He pulsated back and forth through my opening and left me wanting more. We built together our ecstasy until I could hold back no longer. My head swung back. The feeling of a banshee in heat overcame me. The release of passion came to us together as all thought left me except for my lord's pleasure. I fell upon him as it left me, his member still inside.

"I am yours, my lord."

"If you can do that to me every night, I am yours always, my lady."

I leaned onto his chest, still embraced with his shaft in me. "Always, my lord. Promise me something."

"Anything, my lady."

"Tell me you'll always love me."

"Always. Come what may, I will always love you." I fell upon him, his arms wrapping around me as he still kept his size within me.

We took to finding each other during the day. A fortnight passed with us finding corners to be together. Often, I found these the best ways to be taken. But it didn't last for long.

One afternoon, we met near the general area of the pantries. He pulled me in an embrace, leading me to a small door. It was the entrance into a storage chamber. He closed it quickly before anyone saw where we had gone. He locked it behind him to give us our safety. Surrounded by storage chests for the castle, he kissed my shoulders and moved aside my chemise to grab at my breasts below my bodice.

I leaned back, letting him fondle as much as he wished. He had me body and soul. I couldn't refuse him. The sounds on the other side of the closet door had us freeze in our attentions to each other. Our eyes looked to the door. The fear built my feelings of passion. The thought of being caught made me want to kiss and feel my lord's lips upon me more. I wanted to be taken if we were found.

But we weren't at that moment. I remember sighing, and we carried on with caresses as he lifted my bodice and my overdress from my shoulders. I stood before him in my chemise and undergarments. He came towards me, lifting his kilt to take me in the confines of the storage chamber. My heart beat suddenly when I realized his intentions. I thrust my lips upon his mouth, reaching under his kilt for him to find me sooner.

He laid me gently to the ground, pushing up my chemise to gain access to my creamy opening. The length of my thighs could feel his strong pressure as he leaned over me. "I can't hold myself back when I see you."

"Nor I." I leaned back as he held me, pinning me to the floor. Upon me, his kisses covered my face as I felt him enter me. The explosion of pleasure as he entered drew my breath. He thrust hard, hungry for my womanhood lips around his shaft. That's when we heard the key in the storage door lock.

We paused for only a moment. Only one other person had a key to all of the storage rooms. Auntie. Our eyes locked as I remembered our promise to each other. I answered his thoughts in an instant with a whisper. If this was our downfall, I only had one thought left. I whispered to him, "I want to feel you inside me, Conall."

He thrust into me. I thought of nothing but the ravishing of my lord, bringing me to a point that I could not think.

Auntie's scream drowned out our passion as we came together.

Highlander Bride Freedom

Scottish Erotic Tales Book 3

Chapter 1

June 7, 1712

We met near the castle's pantries. Conall pulled me into an embrace, leading me to a small door. It was the entrance into a storage chamber. He closed it quickly before anyone saw where we had gone. He locked it behind him to give us our privacy. Surrounded by storage chests for the castle, he kissed my shoulders and moved aside my chemise to grab at my breasts below my bodice.

I leaned back, letting him fondle as much as he wished. He had me body and soul. I couldn't refuse him. The sounds on the other side of the closet door had us freeze in our attentions to each other.

Our eyes looked to the door. The fear built my feelings of passion. The thought of being caught made me want to kiss and feel my lord's lips upon me. I wanted to be taken if we were found.

He came towards me, lifting his kilt to take me in the confines of the storage chamber. My heart beat suddenly when I realized his intentions. I thrust my lips upon his mouth, reaching under his kilt for him to find me sooner.

He laid me gently to the ground, pushing up my chemise to gain access to my creamy opening. The length of my thighs could feel his strong pressure as he leaned over me.

He breathed deeply, pulling at my lips. "I can't hold myself back when I see you."

"Nor I." I leaned back as he held me, pinning me to the floor. His kisses covered my face as I felt him enter me. The explosion of pleasure as he thrust faster and faster drew my breath. He thrust into me hard, hungry for my womanhood lips around his shaft. That's when we heard the key in the storage door lock.

We paused for only a moment. Only one other person had a key to all of the storage rooms. Auntie. Our eyes locked as I remembered our promise to each other. If this was our downfall, I only had one thought left. I answered his thoughts in an instant with a whisper. "I want to feel you inside me, Conall."

He thrust into me. I thought of nothing but the ravishing of my lord, bringing me to the point that I could not think.

Auntie's scream drowned out our passion as we came together.

Her voice was filled with motherly rage. "Conall, are you mad? Here among the castle storage? Our new lady deserves better than this."

We froze. Auntie picked up my overdress and handed it to me. "Hide behind those barrels until I say to come out. That scream will be sure to bring someone."

Out of breath, Conall had to help lift me from the floor. Hay was stuck in my hair and around my shoulders as I pulled my chemise down. He guided me behind the barrels at the back of the storage chamber. He put himself in front of me, shielding any sight of me since I still only wore my chemise. My heart beat faster as I heard footsteps running. Not heavy boots, but the slight taps of a woman's shoes.

"My lady? Are you all right?" A small servant girl ran from around the corner.

"Tis' nothing but a large rat. Biggest I have ever seen down here. Just startled me 'tis all." Auntie waved at the servant girl's questions.

"Now be back to your work. I'll bring up some of the good brandy his lordship asked for. Thank you for paying such good attention for me. Now, scoot."

She turned her about and gave her a pat on the bum to move. She didn't hesitate. We heard her footsteps echo down the corridor. It brought a sigh of relief when I heard the footsteps echo no more.

"You can come out now."

We eased out of our hiding place. Auntie had her hands firmly on her hips. "What do you think you two are doing, taking your attentions towards each other to such lengths. You could be discovered."

"You knew of us being together?" My voice broke in disbelief.

"Well yes. My brother couldn't bed a sheep at eighty-one years. He has no urges left within him. I was expecting the McPhersons to marry their daughter to you." She points a finger at my beloved. "But they are more observers of tradition than us. I couldn't argue. But I saw the way he looked at you, and you at him on the wedding night."

She came closer and pushed us together. "I know true love when I see it. It was just like my Sarah. She was destined for another, but found someone more true to her. When she learned she couldn't be with him, she jumped from the castle tower." She clasped my hand, patting it gently. "I couldn't let that happen to you, my dear."

"What are we to do? I love him, Auntie." I tried to keep back the sob growing in my gut.

"I know, my dear. But my brother is old. If some babe is born of your union, it will be believed to be your husband's. I doubt he has consummated anything though. Am I right?"

I shook my head "no" in answer. She continued. "I thought so. No, it is better to have an heir, especially a strong one from my grandson." She turned to my beloved. "Conall, you must be more careful. Being together in the castle can be dangerous. Rides are safer. Many a babe has been born to a lord with a ride about his lands. You can take the new lady to inspect her new home, and no one will fault you guarding her tent."

"Aye. You are right." He eyed me with a mischievous smile. "I must protect our family's new lady."

"Take men loyal to you Conall, and ride the lands. You need to inspect them right now anyway." She turned to me. "And that should give you some time together to make sure Clan McFarris has an heir." She winked at me.

I couldn't help but throw my arms around her and hug her dearly. "I will try my best."

"And it is fun trying." She winked at me. "Now, go." This time she swatted me on the arse. "Take your lord to see your new homeland."

Chapter 2

It felt good to be seated on a horse again. I'd missed riding. I thought I'd be shut up mostly in a castle with my new life. I breathed in the fresh air, savoring the smell of trees and earth. Being surrounded by stone the rest of my life wasn't what I was suited for. I was a part of the land.

I gazed forward to see my Lord Conall seated astride his horse. His kilt spilled to the side, revealing his wool riding trews. He was a master horseman, his men following his every instruction. He looked so strong, in command, controlling in his mastery of his horse. I wanted him to take charge of me.

I looked behind to see if my lady-in-waiting was keeping up. Conall had insisted I bring only one lady since he wanted to keep the survey party small and able to maneuver the high country. She was one of the younger girls that attended me, and fast becoming a friend. Mary was her name, and I was starting to look forward to our time in the evenings when we'd catch up about our day.

I looked back ahead to see Conall sitting high in the saddle, rising in the stirrups and raising his fist high in the sign to stop the progression of the party.

"This looks like a good place to set up camp for the evening." He turned to me. "If you permit me, my Lady, we'll set up your tent by those trees there. The lads will make a ring of their bedding. I'll set up a cot near the entrance to your tent, if you don't mind. I want to make sure you and your lady-in-attendance are safe."

"That sounds reasonable, my lord. Thank you." I nodded in his direction, and he nodded back with his mischievous grin. It would be our first night together outside the castle. I was looking forward to sharing furs with him on our good land.

I swung off the horse. "Mary, unpack my things. I'll join you after I take my mare down to the creek to quench her thirst."

I led my horse to the creek near the campsite. My hand would brush against her soft muzzle as we walked. I eyed the area around our campsite. This was a lovely, relaxing place to stop. Foxgloves were in bloom along the edge. The trickle of the water near the edge was calming.

I could see the large green of the hills around us with white flowered hawthorn bushes dotted among the other shrubs tucked around the animal paths from the main road.

A slight breeze brought the gentle hint of the hawthorn to my nose. I took a moment to enjoy the solitude and serenity. I lost track of time until I saw one of the men from the camp come down one of the animal trails.

Conall's man came up and took the reins of my mount. "I'll take care of her, my Lady. Go rest. I'm sure this rough terrain is hard for you to get used to."

"I am a highlander, my Lord. I was born in the saddle."

"Yes, my lady. I can see that. Most ladies would have begged my lord to stop way back. He was testing you." He leaned to me. "I think you passed."

I tried to not blush. "Thank you, Lord Duncan. I do love to ride. It was good to get out of the castle."

"Tis' the time of year to be out, Lady McFarris." He bowed, and led my horse back to be with the others.

I pulled my cloak around me to keep the chill of the late afternoon at bay. I walked back up the trail to the camp.

Mary came up to me with a smile from ear to ear. I had to ask her the reason. "Tell me what has happened. It must be good news."

A glint was in her eyes as she spoke. "He says he fancies me."

My heart skipped. She had her heart set on Conall's second-in-command, Duncan. I grabbed her shoulders. "Really? Then you must go see if you can sup with him later tonight."

"But my lady, I must serve you."

"I'll be fine. I can have Lord Conall join me for my meal. I can't stand in the way of my lady's happiness. Please, break bread with him. And give me the details when you are done. You will owe me that as my lady."

Her face broke with such happiness. "You are truly a saint. Thank you."

She turned and went to join Lord Duncan, the man seeing to the horses that had met me at the creek. He clasped her hand and kissed it. I couldn't help but smile. I knew how much it meant to be with the one you loved.

I turned and headed to the tent that had been erected for my comforts. It was a simple canvas camp tent, with a slight overhang in the front held up with posts. I relished the comfort it gave, and the respite it gave from prying eyes. I had to be careful to step around the guide ropes staking it down. I slowly moved aside the tent flap to enter.

Conall's men mostly had kept to themselves the last two days. Conall had to keep up appearances during the trip so far until he was sure that the distance between home and our location was safe away from others he did not trust. I had been waiting, longing with desire, keeping up appearances.

Tonight, he had promised to not keep his distance. We had been so careful since our discovery by Auntie. I knew it was wise to act such. But I so longed to caress his chest, taste the saltiness of his skin, and have him plunge into my depth. I almost could wait no longer.

I walked into the tent and saw the men had already placed my trunk down, set out the wooden folding table and chairs, and I could smell the cooking of stew over a campfire. Mary had set my things about the tent making it feel like a home.

Everyone had made things very comfortable as I'd been visiting through the countryside. Several of the villages were out to see me astride my horse, the new lady of the castle on display. I would nod, talk to the farmers, and try to be as friendly as possible. I noticed Conall smiling as I talked with his people, now mine.

I had just enough time to take off my riding gloves and set my things in order when Conall walked in. He more than walked; he strode into the room, coming up to me bent over my trunk. He scooped me up in his arms. The sweep of it enfolded me in his cloak. "There is no village to stay in tonight. No prying eyes of anyone but people we trust. Tonight, you are mine, my love." He pulled me towards him, his lips finding mine and matching my need as our bodies responded to each other.

He swept his hand over my head, pulling my braid in front, and starting to undo the way I had arranged it for riding. I stopped him. "No, let me, my love."

I stepped away, wanting to show my lord myself in my glory. I undid the braid, loosened the strands, and shook my hair free about my shoulders. His breath stopped. "You take my breath as if you were a banshee. What spell do you have over me, woman?"

"I know not, my love, but just what you see before you. Myself is all I have to give you."

"It is enough." He pulled me close, kissed me, lingering slowly, pulling on my lips. The kisses traveled down the side of my neck, feathering my shoulders as he pulled at the chemise. "I could eat you for my dinner tonight."

"Aye, my Lord. Eat as much of me as you would like."

He kissed me again, and cupped behind my head, pushing my hair away from my face. "My lady Heather, what you do to me! You drive me out of my mind for longing. It has been such a long day in the saddle. All I've been thinking of is being alone with you tonight."

"I, as well, my lord."

We heard someone clear their throat loudly outside the tent flap. "My Lord, we have your meals if you'd allow us to enter."

Conall took his hand away from my face, and stepped back. "You may enter, Lord Hurley." The tent flap lifted, and one of Conall's men stepped in with his squire to lay our bowls of stew and a loaf of bread on the camp table.

He nodded to us, and stepped out. I heard the shuffling of their boots as they left the front of the tent.

Conall moved back towards me. He kissed me again. "I guess it was decided that we should eat first."

"I am hungry, Conall. But for more than just food. Satisfying that craving first will help me enjoy the second sevenfold."

"By all means my lady, I will quench your thirst and hunger for good wine and stew. Then I'll see to your other needs. I promise." He pulled me close, and I could feel his manhood hard against me promising he would see to my body later. I kissed him, and pulled his hand towards the table. "You must eat as well. I don't want you suffering from lack of energy."

"I have no lack of energy. I am running on the energy you spur me to feel when I look at you."

I sat down at the table, broke a piece of bread off to dip in the stew. "What compels you so, Conall?"

"My good lady, your lips seduce me while you speak. Your hands ravish me with your movements. Your hips beg me to take you. I am lost without being close to you."

I drank some of the wine from the flask. "I love it when you say my name, Conall."

"Heather. My beautiful flower of a woman. My dear lady Heather, you rule my heart."

I dipped my bread in the stew and took a bit. "But how many flowers have you picked before me to know of the workings of a woman?"

"Enough that you should know that a bouquet is more beautiful with nurturing. I want to nurture you, and plant an heir within you. Over and over until we are sure you are bearing." He took a deep bite of his bread. "I'll be glad to see him born."

"How do you know the babe will be a boy? There could be a girl born first."

"Rarely are girls born first to the McFarris clan. In several generations back, the firstborn has always been a boy."

I got up and retrieved my wine skin, offering it to Conall after I'd taken a long draught. My mind was swirling with the effects of the wine, making me feel more randy than ever before.

The berry taste of the red swirled through my mouth. It was making me feel bold. "You, I'm sure, will plant within me a fine son. I have no doubt."

He grabbed me and pulled me into his lap. "And again, and again, so help me. I will never be able to keep my hands off you."

He grabbed my breast, and I smacked him with my slice of bread. I couldn't help but play with him a bit. I was feeling powerful. Denial would torture him. "Eat first. Remember, you need your strength for the heir begetting."

He took the bowl and a large piece of bread, slathered it with stew and took a mouthful. I gave him the skin and he took a long drink. I took the skin after him, savoring the deep red taste, the oak flavor tangy on my tongue. "All day I've been thinking of what I would do to you, Conall."

His eyebrow rose as he stuffed more stew-filled bread into his mouth. "What is it you've been planning?"

I took the skin. "I've thought about what you've taught me in the ways of marriage, my lord." I held the bottom of the skin, and wrapped my mouth around the nozzle forming my lips into a perfect "O".
 I suckled the end, and then moved the skins tip up and down, simulating my last pleasuring of my lord's manhood. His eyes widened and he slapped his knee. "My Heather is a quick learner."

"I do want to please my lord." I drank more wine, and held the skin to my lord to drink from. He looked at me, locking eyes, as he drank from the skin. "I have plans too, my love. I imagine your perky breasts, your round nipples, hard from my caresses, and your back arching as I take you again so hard we feel the pleasure between us together."

I lean down, and he takes the wine skin out of my hands, placing it on the table. He starts unlacing the front of my riding bodice, the laces slipping away to let my breasts appear from underneath my chemise. Conall pulls the leather cord out, and lets it hang to the side as his hands disappear into the folds of my chemise. I feel his questing hand find my breasts. My nipples pebble as his hands find them under the chemise. "Come to me, woman."

I lean towards him, balancing on his knee so his head can lean into my bosom. I let him bury his lips into my fleshy folds, taking his head and cradling it to my breasts. He finds one and sucks it, building my sensations that travel down to my toes through my toes.

I lean back, holding his head as he suckles me like the child he'll soon place in me. He pushes up my skirts, reaching under them stroking my thighs. My mind builds with lust. "Conall, take me. I have waited so long for you to be in me again."

He picks me up, smiles, and carries me to the mound of sleeping furs and blankets. "Aye, my love. You can count on it."

He lowers me into the nest of wool blankets and furs assembled on my sleeping pallet. I cannot stop staring into his brown eyes. I am lost joining in his look of lust and love. I want to feel him on top of me so much I pull him on me when he places me on the pallet. He chuckles. "Hold there, my lady. I'll topple upon you if you're not careful."

"I want to be covered with you, Conall. A blanket of Scottish man."

"I will gladly cover you always, my love."

He leans down over me, kissing me, burning my lips into a sensation of passion I'd not felt before. He pulls me up to him, pulling off my bodice and sleeves, placing them to the side of the bed. He unpins his kilt from his shoulder and it falls to his side.

I watch the marvel of my lord reveal his manly shape in stages of glory only reserved for his lady. He stands to unfasten his belt and let his kilt drop to the floor. He unlaces his shirt and draws it over his head. Before me is the glory of my lord, his bare chest worked into chiseled strength by his swordplay.

He unwraps the string that holds up his trews, dropping them down into the pile of wool. His glorious wavy brown hair falls to below his shoulders as he unties the thong that held it. I sigh. He stands before me, his manhood erect and ready to take me.

He kneels down over me, caressing the valley between my breasts and I close my eyes. He pulls me towards him, kissing me, and I get my body to will itself to him. I submit to my lord fully and utterly in body and mind.

He holds me, and I feel the need to hold still as he pulls my skirts and pantaloons down. I lift my bum so he could guide them downward off my body. He pulls me back up and lifts my chemise over my head, placing it to the side. I lay before him in my woman's glory, naked and ready to be taken again. He crawls back to be lingering above me, taking in the sight of my naked body. "My God, woman, you are heaven on Earth."

"Aye, my Lord. You are heaven to me as well."

He leans back onto me, enslaving my body to him by his touch. His lips travel down between my breasts, taking time to suckle each one. He nuzzles my nipples to make my back arch with need. My womanhood grows wet in readiness for his seed. His kisses travel to my stomach, kissing feathers, caressing my navel, and down my hips to my thighs.

He pushes my legs apart, and looks at me. "Are you ready, woman?"

"Yes my lord. Make me yours."

I watch him lean down between my legs, and close my eyes to enjoy his attentions. I feel the sensations of pleasure travel up my thighs, making me throb into a frenzy as he sucks on my womanhood over and over. I spread my legs for him, and I feel his tongue plunge into me.

My head lolls back. Over and over he sends his tongue into me, building me into a lustful wench that overtakes my being. Spasms overtake my body as he lets the passion spill over. It takes me, ravaging my core and my very being until I relax in a state of bliss for only him.

"Did you enjoy that, lass?"

It took a moment for me to recover from my lord's ravishing attentions. "Aye, my Lord. You can do that to me every night. I serve only as your woman."

"I intend to do that to you often. But there are other ways to please you."

"I am but your servant. Always." I lean back, opening my legs to him, ready to receive. I was hungry for his seed. Hungry for his heir. He sits up, and I see the look in his eye. It is of such longing and lust. I have to lean back in the furs more, opening my legs more, wanting his thrusts to rock my being. "I await your lord's pleasure."

He eases his manhood toward my opening. He feels the edges of my lusty flower, sending tendrils of lust down my thighs. His movements open my petals to receive his shaft. He thrusts into me, and I open my legs to take him in fully. Again and again he thrusts into me, rocking me on the furs that cradle our lovemaking.

He plunges into me over and over, rocking back and forth atop me, causing the sensations to build again. He moves straight over my wet site of heaven to build me to release. The pleasure causes my head to snap back in lust.

I let it wash over me until I cannot think of nothing but his shaft in me. I shudder with the lust for him. I feel him do the same before collapsing over me, kissing my lips and my neck to my shoulders. He wraps his arms around me as I crawl closer. I pull his face towards me, kissing his lips, tasting myself on his mouth. I want the lust we'd spent within us to be a babe. So much it hurt. I want our baby to hold and love.

He rolls to my side, and I move to lie across him, not wanting to loose the connection between us. My womanhood pulses with his impassioned thrusts, wanting to engage in some more play, hoping his manhood would turn into a sword again to take me. I wasn't done yet. I was becoming greedy in my lust for him.

"My Lord knows how to please me." I kiss him, savoring the scent of his manly body; the smell of him was intoxicating. I wanted more, but knew not if he would let me. We lay with our breathing talking between us. Over and over, I lost the thought of everything but just laying next to my lord. All my thoughts and hopes were nothing without him.

When I noticed his breathing had slowed, he wrapped his arms around me pulling me close. I smiled. I had an idea. Something that would appeal to the horsewoman within me. "My lord, I have an idea."

"Yes?"

"I'm not done yet."

"Really?"

"I think I'd like to master you as a steed."

"You are a masterful rider, my lady. I am your stallion to tame." He releases me, rolling onto his back, arms spread at my mercy.

I smile, knowing now he was open to my idea. I mount my lord, taking command of his shaft. I position it to my wet opening, rolling the head and submerging it with my juices. His moans tell me I am accomplishing my goal of mutual pleasure. I position his shaft to kiss my wet, womanhood lips, and thrust him within me. His shaft pushes deep, and I enjoy the sensation of having him again within my depth. His face flushes with pleasure as I feel him captured within me.

I stand upward, using my knees to gain the angle to thrust his member in and out. I lean down and push him within me once more. I feel my feminine lips encapsulate his fullness. Leaning down on him, I kiss him deeply, rubbing myself at our union building the sensations of passion. Again and again, I am a highlander bride feeling her freedom riding her lord.

"Heather, you are a goddess." His face flushes with ecstasy. I know that my taming of my stallion is working. "I want you deep within me, my love." With one more thrust, I angled my hips so I take him deep within the depths of my being for a final thrust. His moan accented the feelings traveling up my very core, sending me into a rush of lust. I began to rub back and forth on his member, enjoying the sensations it causes me to feel. "Oh my lord, you are a prime stallion."

"My lady, take me. I'm all yours!"

I rub against him, over and over as he has done to me. The sensations moved through my being as before. I am now controlling the rush of feelings.

I feel so wonderful, building the urges within me to bang against his hard body, over and over. I feel like a stallion myself claiming my lord. I feel the scream of a banshee ready to be released. "You are mine, Conall. I pledge myself to you. Send your seed into me. I am ready to receive."

I give one last thrust to his member locked within me, his body convulses and I lean into him, feeling myself tighten around him. I know an heir has been blessed within me this night. There was no doubt.

I lay on him, spent from my ride. I still feel the full shaft of my lord within me. I rub against him at the certainty of our union locked together. Then, I feel the loosening of his size as he slips out of me. I let him escape, and lay next him, kissing his nipples and well-formed chest. He is a God of old times laying next to me.

He wraps his arms around me as I crawl up on him like a cat. "Oh, Heather. You are my wicked woman."

"Yes. We have fallen into hell, and are creating our heaven between us."

He rolls on me, and kisses me deeply. "You are my life. Lo, I vow to kill anyone that threatens to separate us."

I grab his face, pulling his lips towards me. "I would die without you."

He lowers his heavenly body, pressing his chest to seal us in a union of heaven on Earth. "Always, my love. I am yours."

His lips seal our promise. I am his. Always. There is no other thing to behold but my lord, and everything else is something to be forgotten. He is my everything.

Chapter 3

I awoke to the sounds of movement around the tent. I turned to reach towards Conall. He was not there. I let me eyes adjust to the darkness, and could see a dark figure by the doorway. As my eyes got used to the dim light of the rising dawn, I could see Conall half dressed, sword in hand, poised by the door flap. I knew that was a sign something was wrong.

He saw me sit up, and put a hand to his lips for silence. I pulled the covers up to my neck, trying to hide my naked form. Danger was clearly lurking outside, and I didn't want it to find us. The flap opened. A man wearing my clans signet walked in and noticed me in the bed. "My Lady, are you Lady McPherson?"

"Who wishes to know?" I wanted to keep the man distracted as I saw Conall ease behind him.

"Your good husband has died, and we had lost contact with you in the country. Your brothers have taken the castle. We feared you had been killed."

Conall came up and grabbed him leveraging his dagger at the man's throat. "What is this that brings you into our camp unannounced?"

The man sneered. "You must be the traitor nephew that abducted the good lady. You want the whole clan to follow you? You had better do something to rectify this tragedy. So far, all are blaming you."

Conall pushed the dagger closer to the man's throat. "How did you get close to here?"

"Had to kill your night watch. Sad fellow. Didn't know much how to use a sword well. I imagine we'll find out how well you know." He thrust back his arm and hit Conall in the stomach. Conall regained his ground, and blocked the sword swing with his dagger. In his other hand, he swung his sword, cutting the legs of his opponent. I held my breath, watching my love cut down the intruder.

The intruder grabbed his sword and rolled to stand, ignoring the wince of pain it took to face Conall again. "You've got to do better than that to stop me."

"It seems to have put a damper on your speed."

The man came at Conall with a high-handed swing. Conall blocked it, and countered with an underhanded slash that was stopped by the other man. Back and forth they swung. The pings of their blades made me anxious for Conall.

I heard other footsteps running outside and saw the tent flap open. Lord Hurley entered and stopped when he saw the fight. He drew his sword and rounded a swing at the man. Cornered, the intruder fought off a swing from both Conall and Lord Hurley. A swing knocked the sword from the intruder's hands.

Holding his sword at the other man's throat, Conall had a look of rage. "Tell me what has happened."

"Lord McFarris has died. Since their lass married to the lord has disappeared, they are assuming she has been killed to destroy the peace between the clans. I suggest, my Lord Conall, we ride back to find out exactly how to stop their tempers before all hell breaks loose between the clans."

Conall reached down and pulled the man up. "I spare you only if you can help us. If all has happened as you say, we've got to return."

85

Turning, he spoke to Lord Hurley. "Take him outside, and tie him up. I don't want him attacking us on the way back. If war does break out between the clans, I don't want his dagger in my back."

Lord Hurley stood, eyeing Conall. "It may take a sacrifice to seal the truce once more. Are you prepared to make it?"

"More than ready." Lord Hurley left with the intruder as Conall noticed me standing wrapped in our sleeping fur. He came and folded me in his arms. "We need to go straighten this situation out with your brothers. I'm hoping they'll keep their word if you live."

He held me for a moment, my trembles from the fighting easing as he caressed my shoulders. I sighed. "I hope my brothers see reason. Right now, you are the Lord McFarris to answer for your clan. Maybe we can talk to them and find a way to bring peace again. Maybe it's a big misunderstanding."

I shook my head. "Or a play for power. They could use this to seize my lands unless I can get back there."

He cupped my face kissing my lips softly. I closed my eyes, enjoying the gentle touch after the brutal force I witnessed before. "We will have to ride hard today. We might be able to make it by sundown if we do not take much time but to water the horses. Do you trust me?"

I looked into his eyes. I was lost in the depths of the brown that I saw. Gentle and loving waves enveloped his face and I couldn't hold back from kissing him back. When we took to breathing again, I said, "Always, my love. I trust you and will follow you to the ends of the Earth."

***

The castle loomed before me again. This time the shadow of the future loomed ahead with something that illuminated it at my side. Conall rode next to me. He felt if my brothers could see I was with him, they would understand that this was all a tragic sad event of timing. Always enemies lurked to take advantage of such a situation. I was determined to help Conall straighten this one out and avoid the bloodshed that was threatening to erupt around us. I wanted to hold his hand, and looked at him.

His smile warmed me. "Are you nervous?"

I shook my head, my braid swinging at my back. "No. I was just remembering the last time I traveled up this embankment. The view of the castle was the sign of my marital doom. I almost threw myself out of the carriage to avoid my fate."

His look of chagrin was my reward for staying in the carriage. "I'm glad you chose to live."

"So am I. But it is different this time."

"Why?"

I looked at his angular face and jawline with the hint of stubble. I sighed. I couldn't help but fall in love with him all over again. "I have you at my side. I do not want to be separated. I want to stay with you. Whatever fate we meet at the end of this path, I want to meet it together."

"As always, my love. I'd sooner die than be parted from you now."

He stopped and reached for me. Our horses reined in at our command, and we held hands. The whole movement of our party stopped as he lifted my hand to his lips, and kissed the outer part of my riding glove. It was our first outward sign of our affections in public. I felt my heart beat faster. Displaying our love in public was a risk.

He lowered my hand. "Are you ready to face our future?"

"Yes, my love."

We reached the gate and were ushered in by the guards wearing McFarris and McPherson garb. I rose steady in the saddle, smiling at the men. They nodded back. A very good sign. I was hoping my presence would be the white dove of peace. I knew it had always been my duty and sacrifice to marry for peace. What would I have to sacrifice this time to save my clansmen and Conall?

Our hooves clattered into the courtyard. Their sounds echoed off the stones as we saw people assembling ahead to receive us. No swords were drawn, but men warily hovered their hands near their belts. Thumbs postured in the air, ready to clamp onto steel. The hairs on the back of my neck started to stand on end. Things were going to happen very quickly. I had to remain calm and settle my mind to say the right words.

Conall came forward and dismounted his horse. He went to the other side of mine and helped me down. He drew me towards the assembled people, holding my hand in a regal way before my oldest brother, Lionel.

My brother Lionel stepped down into the courtyard in front of me. His boar-like face grimaced at the whole party. "Are you all right, Heather?"

"Yes, Lionel. I am fine. I have heard the sad news of my husband's passing. It grieves me I was not here, but away getting to know the land and his people so I may better serve his household. I will do my duty and make my way to him now."

Lionel held up his hand. "Hold good sister. There is but one problem. If you are now a widow, it means that the McFarris Clan is not joined to us by marriage. There is, as yet, no heir of the union. Since not but a month has passed, we may not know of the likelihood of an heir for a while. This union was to hold the truce between clans."

He turned to Conall and bowed slightly before speaking. "My Lord, you are now the clan chief by blood rites. You are his nephew and the only living heir of Clan McFarris. I ask you now, how do you plan to make this right? How do you intend to hold this truce?"

Conall strode before Lionel, and did a turn. I could see heads peeking out of windows looking into the courtyard to listen. People were spilled from the doorways onto the cobble steps to gain a listen to what he was to say.

Conall cleared his throat. "My Lord McPherson." He rolled his shoulders back to stand tall. "I plan to keep the truce by the way it was planned in the first place. A marriage. I will marry Lady McPherson to continue the lasting peace between our two clans."

My heart missed a beat. It fluttered in my throat as Conall continued. He came towards my brother and slapped him on the back. "Aye. And I promise you, my good lord, a fine heir to be born by this time next year."

With his last words, cheers erupted through the courtyard. People yelled and clapped from all around us. But I was unable to focus on it. All I could see was Conall's brown eyes drawing me to him. I ran and flung myself into his arms, and he grabbed me up, kissing me deeply.

My brother laughed and shook his head when we drew apart. "I am guessing my lady sister agrees to this."

I turned to him, still encircled in Conall's arms. "Of course, dear brother. We must keep the peace. It is my duty to marry into the McFarris clan."

Lionel laughed. "Then, it's time to plan another wedding. Unless we drank all the ale at the last one?"

Still holding me, Conall turned to my brother. "Of course not. I saved the good ale further down in the cellars so no one would know of it. That is what we'll drink for the second McFarris wedding this summer."

I turned to Conall and smiled. "And this time, we'll make extra sure there's enough wine and ale for all so no one need drink the river."

Everyone laughed at my jest. I reached up and kissed the man I loved, feeling freedom for the first time since I'd arrived at Castle McFarris. We were free to love each other now, forever.

Seduction Of A Highlander

Erotic Fay Tale Book 1

Chapter 1

April 8, 1730

CLARA the Nymph

I saw a group of Scottish warriors coming through my glen--strapping men, the kind I wanted to lay down and take roughly through the night. They were dressed in kilts and leather armor, and were carrying two-handed broadswords. I hid in the trunk of my tree, concealing my form into its bulk so they couldn't see me. But I could see them. Maybe I could convince them to stay with me.

I noticed a younger lad in the group. His long brown hair was held back with a leather thong. The strap was loose, letting his hair come undone and frame his stubbled face. I leaned forward with a breath of a whisper, "Stay with me." I felt him reach for my hand, which was disguised as a branch.

He stopped, looked around, and shouted, "Father, what about this place for the night?"

A heavyset man at the front turned to look at the lad. "Why would you say that, Hamish?"

"This seems like a good place to settle. The sun is going down, and we could mount a guard over there." He pointed at a large outcrop of rock near my glen. "We could set someone there to watch easily. A fire in the center of the glen would be hidden by the thick trees. It seems like a good spot for the night."

The man the boy had called "father" wore the pin of a chief. The pin fastened his tartan over his shoulder. He put his hands on his hips. "Aye." He looked around my trees, setting his eyes on my home tree. I sent a breeze to convince him to stay. I wrapped my ethereal arms around his waist, sending my spirit to pull at his kilt. "A bit windy here."

"But a stable area to guard." An older man came up beside the lad. His gray hair moved in my breeze. "The lad is right, Conall. We need a place to camp. This is as good as any if we kept going."

"All right, Brian. We'll stop here for the night," spoke Chief Conall.

Brian turned to the lad and put a hand on his shoulder. "You have sharp eyes. We'll make you into a commander yet."

"Thank you, McFarland."

I watched the chief turn back and head into my glen. He gave the order for the men to stop, and the warriors breathed sighs of relief at finally being able to lower their packs to the ground. Each got to the job of setting up camp quickly. Two of the men set off to gather wood.

One man started to unload some basic cooking pots for a meal. One warrior lowered a large bow and started checking the arrows. The lad lowered his pack and took in the scenery around him. He stared right at my tree for a moment, taking a moment to look at me. Then shook his head, and got to unpacking.

One of the men next to Hamish whispered, "I'm glad you mentioned stopping. The chief would have kept pushing us. He knows it's unlucky to keep going through the woods in the dark."

Hamish socked him in the arm. "Come on, Dougal. You're not scared of the dark woods, are you?"

"Not of the woods, but what might come out in the dark. They say these are fairy woods."

"A warrior scared of the fay? How can you believe they are real?"

"How can you believe there are none? Strange things do happen here." He looked around. "I hope we leave early in the morning. I don't know how well I'll be sleeping tonight." He looked back at Hamish and winked. "Most likely with one eye open."

"They can't hurt you." Hamish seemed to brush off the idea with his words. "Fay, that is. Most are nice if you have kindness in your heart."

"You've been listening too much to ya Ma. I know there are things watching us even now." He looked around and focused his attention on the trunk of my tree.

I tried not to move, wondering if this man had the sight. I couldn't be too sure. It would make any surprises harder for me if he could see my true form.

The lad brushed if off with a shake of his head and kept unloading his pack. He started spreading his bedroll of furs, and straightened them next to the other man's roll. "Dougal, there's nothing in these woods."

He smoothed out his bedding, and then looked back at the older man. "Besides, the more you talk about it, the more you'll scare yourself. Nothing here but critters natural to the forest. I'd be more afraid of a badger eating your toes than some fay."

Dougal shrugged his shoulders. "Suit yourself. But I'm going to make sure I've got my protection amulet out and ready to fight off any fay that want to bed me while I sleep. They're famous for getting pregnant off of any unsuspecting men that venture into their woods."

I frowned as the man made it clear he knew my plan. I could feel his amulet of protection from where I stood. He would definitely not be a target for me tonight. But the young man, in the prime of his youth, was shaping into a better option for me.

The younger man, Hamish, laughed. "Let them come. I would welcome any fay that wished me to share their bed."

"Watch what you say, lad. They may be listening."

I smiled. I knew I had chosen wisely when I saw this Hamish. Now to wait for evening to put the rest of my plan into action. Yes. He would be perfect. "I want you to know my real name," I whispered.

He looked around, eyes going wide. "What is it?"

"Clara." As I spoke my true name, I felt the spell that would make him mine forever encircle us. I saw his smile and nod. I knew tonight would be our time together.

***

I waited until after their meal, when the fire had gone down. They posted a guard at the outcrop, but I knew that my breath could put him to sleep easily. I came out of my trunk and took my true form. My nymph body formed as I emerged from the tree. Leaves were wrapped within the curls of my blonde tresses. My breasts moved with my lithe form. My bare feet crunched the leaves. I needed to retain some of the tree itself to keep my form.

I sent a breeze to help the guard slumber, and moved to the furs of the sleeping lad, Hamish. The guard slumped at his post. I looked towards Hamish.

His face looked peaceful in slumber, with the faint trace of stubble around his chin. Finally in flesh form, I could touch him. He didn't flinch, but breathed deeply. I felt the pull of his mind in sleep. I leaned down, brushing my lips in a feather touch against his. My naked breasts swayed over him, brushing against the furs escaping from his sleeping pallet. Goosebumps trembled over my skin. My nipples hardened.

I wanted him. To take him here. But I knew it wouldn't be easy to keep us quiet. I needed to have him plant his seed deep inside me to create my heir for my tree. Too bad he would slowly waste away longing for me. But there was no other way to create my daughter. I knew I would need to wake him and draw him from the other men.

I moved closer, leaning against his body, molding myself to him as his eyes fluttered open. He started to gasp. I imposed my will to freeze him. I didn't want to come to harm. But I needed him to cooperate. I caressed his face, relaxing my spell to let him move.

I put my finger to his lips and whispered, "Your fellow warrior was right. These woods are full of fay. I am one, as you see. A fairy come to be with you for one night." He gasped as I put a finger to his lips. "All I ask is for a night together, and never to be heard from again. Come with me, and I will show you pleasures beyond your dreams."

He blinked once, trying to focus on me. "Are you a dream?" He tried to sit up.

I leaned over him. "No. I will show you how real I am."

I pressed my lips against his, waiting for him to kiss back, certain of his acceptance. There was a pause, and I leaned back. "Do you not want me?"

His hands rose to wrap around me. "I feel an undeniable pull to you." He blinked again. "Yes. I want to be with you."

I could feel his hesitation. His fear. I kissed him again, pulling on his lips in my sweet seduction. This time, he kissed back. I melted into his embrace, feeling his arms pull me towards him. We moved among his furs, and the man next to him stirred. I stopped and sat up. "We must move from here, or we will wake the others."

"Where will we go?" His eyes traced down my body.

I smiled at him. "I know of a place." I stroked his strong jaw. His stubble was rough against my touch. "Come with me."

Chapter 2

I led him to the stone sanctuary in the center of my glen. It was an area with a very flat stone, once used as an altar by the druids that often visited me. His hand clutched mine. His eyes were wide as he looked at my naked form and back at the stone slab covered with leaves. "Is this the place?"

"Yes." I leaned into him again, kissing him. My hands explored down his chest, and under his kilt. When my explorations reached his flesh, his kissing grew more passionate. I pulled his tunic over his head, exposing his toned chest and arms strengthened by sword training.

I caressed his muscles as he watched me enjoy his body. His voice questioned my presence. "You can't be real. You must be a dream." I felt his hands circle around my back.

"I assure you, I am very real." I kissed him again and held his hand, leading him to the stone slab. Pulling him to lie upon it, I kneeled over him. "A night with the fay is something that can't be taken for granted." I stroked his hair, pulling it back from his face. "It is a gift and honor to be chosen."

I kissed his forehead, down his cheek to his chest and over the defined bumps of his abdomen. I heard his breaths of pleasure as I tasted the saltiness of his human flesh. I held the edge of his kilt. I moved the material aside as his exposed, hard cock was revealed. "I will give you a reward if you give me what I want."

"And what is it you want?" His look of innocence was charming.

I raised an eyebrow. "First, I will give you your reward." I took his large cock in my mouth, easing it to the back of my throat. I easily wrapped my lips around the base. I eased my mouth back up his shaft, tightening the pressure to give him the most pleasure. My tongue licked and circled his tip, and I grabbed the base of him to play with the sacks as I sucked. Again and again I pulled up and down, building him to the reward I knew I could give him.

"I'm losing myself to you." His hands reached down, and he wrapped his fingers around my locks.

I kept at my attentions, licking the soft skin down the back of his member. I grabbed the root of his shaft and licked along the large vein up the back. I wanted him to grow to his full length so I could take him deep within me.

"What are you doing to me?" His perplexed statement brought me away from his cock.

I leaned down, moving my body over the top of him, rubbing my breasts against his chest. I pulled myself on top of him, and whispered, "Have you not felt this before?"

"I've never been with a woman."

I couldn't help but laugh. My bell-like voice knitted his eyebrows. I caressed his face to calm him. "Do not fear, young one. I am honored to be your first." I kissed him again, rubbing against his strong, hard body. His arms wrapped around me as his mind started to catch up with the passion of his body. "Yes, that's it. You want me as much as I want you, yes?"

"Yes." His rough tone told me about the raw need building within him.

I rubbed against his erection. He groaned with pleasure. I kissed down his chest, angling my body to give him shivers as my lips passed over him. My feathery breath brought his skin to goosebumps. I sat up and took his large member in my hands. He watched me as I rubbed my wet, slick opening over his cock. He let out another moan, and reached for my hips.

I braced one hand against his chest and held his cock with my other hand. "Let me introduce you to the ways of pleasure, my young human. Experience pure bliss." I raised myself up above, and angled his cock to my wet opening. I rubbed his cock against my slick entrance, easing on my knees to push against his rod with my swollen entry. I wiggled my ass, getting the right angle, and slid his cock deep within me. The surprised gasp fed my own lust as I started to move up and down to build our passion.

I rocked on him, up and down, building him again until his breathing grew to gasps. I rocked him inside me, harder and harder, his moans spurring me on. I built our passion, thrusting him up and down inside me. I leaned back and shouted, "Let go and fill me, Hamish." My muscles contracted around his cock, and I let my mind explode with my own release. Shudders shot through me as I felt him join me in his own unleashed lust.

The euphoric moment passed, and I lay on him. He wrapped his arms around me, holding me tightly and burying his face in my hair. I heard him whisper, "I never want to let you go." I felt his breath rising, his heart beating. I closed my eyes to feel the rhythm of this human. I wanted to remember him. He was special. There was something that made me not want to let him go.

I looked into his eyes. "There is something about you. Something that makes me want to do this with you for a lifetime." The connection was electric. I'd never had this experience with a human male before. A bond started to form. I could feel the spell weave around us. Did he have the sight?

"You can do this to me as long as you want," he said.

"But you forget something. It's your turn now." I rolled back onto the stone slab. He took the lead and moved his body over mine. "What would you like to do to me, Hamish?"

"Everything." He kissed me and covered my body with his own. His heart beat fast as he kissed me. I could feel him growing harder, ready for another round.

I pulled him closer. "Take me Hamish. I am yours tonight."

He kissed my lips, caressing and exploring my body. I could feel the need growing in him again. His lust was pushing against my leg. The calluses on his hands were rough against my breasts as he cupped them. I closed my eyes, and felt his tongue lick my nipples. I sighed as he sucked at my breast. Lightening shot through my body. This boy was quickly becoming a man. I appreciated his natural ability to send waves of pleasure through my body as he nuzzled down my neck and stroked down my sides.

I opened my legs for him as he began to mount me. "I want to take you deep again, Hamish. Bury yourself in me," I moaned.

His growl answered my desire. His cock kissed my slick opening, and he pushed in. "More Hamish," I yelled. "Deeper. Faster."

He thrust in me, and I arched my back to take him fully. Again, he launched into me, pulling out to drive in his next stroke. Again and again, I moved my hips up to receive him, feeling his seed ready to become mine. "More. Fill me."

One final thrust made me release the desire he had built within me. Our shudders roared through our bodies, allowing me to finally have again what I needed.

Several matings would make sure I had an heir. All night he had to be mine. I smiled as I felt the swirls of our bond hold us together. He would not leave me now.

I let him collapse on me, holding me while he was still inside. He kissed my nose, my neck, my lips. "I am yours, beloved."

I caressed his cheek. "Yes, Hamish. I will call you mine."

***

THE NEXT MORNING

"He's not here, Chief." Dougal scratched his head. "He was right next to me when we bedded down for the night. His furs are here, but he is not."

Brian shook his gray head. "I'm sure he's just wondered off somewhere, Conall. He'll be back soon."

The chief sighed heavily. Frustration crossed his voice. "Let's have some of you just take a look around. I need to get him back here so we can carry on with our hunt. We have some distance to cover today."

Brian pointed at some of the men, and they began to fan out calling for Hamish. Conall looked at Brian. "I've been too easy on him. Maybe I should have been tougher. He wouldn't have wandered off then."

"No, this isn't like him, Conall." Brian looked around. "I have the feeling something has happened."

A look of concern crossed the chief's face. "My son should know better than to wander off."

"I think he had help, Chief."

They heard one of the warriors rushing back. Both the older men turned their heads to see Dougal run up. "They found him. He was lying asleep on some rock slab. But they can't rouse him."

"Take me to him." Conall didn't break his stride as he followed Dougal. They crashed through the underbrush to a clearing with rock formations creating a circle. On the center stone slab was Hamish with several men surrounding him. Conall tried to still his heart. He looked directly at one of his men. "Is he dead?"

"He's still breathing, my lord. But he will not rouse."

"Pick him up. We'll have to delay the journey for now, and return back to the castle." He moved forward and caressed Hamish's brow. His son didn't stir. "It's like he's under a spell."

"He may be." Dougal looked around. "These woods are haunted, my lord."

"You there, carry him back." Conall pointed at some of his men. They reached for the young man, pulling his body off the slab and holding him up by his arms. One man grabbed his feet, and another hoisted him around his shoulders. They braced him and began to walk back to the trail.

"We'll get him home Conall." Brian placed his hand on his shoulder. "I'm sure we've got a wise woman that can help."

"I pray we do. I cannot lose my son and heir, Brian."

"Aye." Brian followed behind Conall as the other men carried Hamish. Dougal stopped for moment. He swore he could hear laughter in the breeze. He shook his head a moment, and followed behind the other men.

***

"It's a spell, my lady." The wise woman bent over Hamish. She moved her hands over his body, a mere inch of space between them as she scanned with her palms. Her eyes were closed as she spoke. "His energy is weak, and his heart is growing weaker as well. It's as if something has a hold of it. A darkness surrounds his heart."

113

Lady McFarris had a look of concern written on her tense face. "What can we do?"

The old woman opened her eyes. "Pray for a miracle. This is love magic since it involves the heart. And only love can break the spell. He may wake sometime soon, or never. Only time will tell."

"Is there nothing else to be done?" Lady McFarris didn't hide the fear in her voice.

The old woman looked at her. "I was there to bring him into the world. I know this is not his time. I can feel the strength in him. It's as if he's waiting for something." She stretched her hand to the lady. "You must be strong too. You have before. Something will come that will give us a sign of what to do. Have faith."

The old woman got up and straightened her skirts. "For now, keep him comfortable. Have someone stay with him at all times to monitor his breathing. If there is a change, call me back. Until then," she patted Lady McFarris's hand, "we wait."

Lady McFarris nodded as the wise woman took her leave. Bowing, the woman turned and left the room. Lady McFarris turned to one of her ladies-in-waiting. "I will begin the first watch over my son. From then on, we will take turns." The two ladies standing beside her nodded.

One left the room to pass Lady McFarris's instructions to the staff at the castle. The other brought a chair for her, and took another for herself to sit next to her.

Lady McFarris leaned towards her son's body. She caressed his handsome cheek. His eyelids fluttered for a moment, and her heart skipped a beat. Then he settled into whatever dreams or nightmares were in his mind. She held back the tears as she held his hand. "All we need is a miracle."

Chapter 3

April 24, 1730

MARY of the Village McFarris

I had made my way home when I heard of what had happened to my lord and heir, Lord McFarris. His plight had spread through the McFarris lands. Word was out that they were seeking anyone to try to bring the lad from his fretful sleep. I had heard that many had tried over the last fortnight.

Now, I had come to the castle to try my luck. Music always brought peace to any troubled soul. I'd been playing since I was a small lass. I could still remember playing in the village at festivals. That is when I first met his lordship as a boy.

I'd known him since we were both young. His blue eyes and dark, brown hair had always distinguished him as a McFarris. He held himself like a young lord.

But he was always fair when he played with the village children. I respected him for that.

I could still picture him smiling while trying to tag my younger sister Elena. He had let her get him. She had been thrilled for days.

I knew I had to try to help.

I walked up to the wooden portcullis waiting for anyone to challenge or greet me. A breeze blew some of my red hair from my scarf, and it whipped into my eyes. I quickly tucked it behind my ear. There was movement at the gate, and I heard a voice shout, "Who goes there?"

"I'm the harpist Mary seeking to make Lord McFarris's son rise from his slumber."

I heard the stomping of boots, and a man walked up to the grate of the portcullis. "You've come to try your luck with the lad?" The guard looked me up and down. "The harpist then? Let me see your instrument." I swung my harp case to sit on the ground. Opening it, I lifted my precious wooden instrument so the guard could see. He nodded. "Hope you can do something. No one here has been in their right mind since this all happened. They're saying the lad is cursed."

The chain started to creak as the man stepped back. The gate rose. I stepped underneath, swinging the harp into place again on my back. The leather strap rested around my shoulder. The guard turned to me. "I'll escort you through the courtyard to the lady of the keep. Lady McFarris is meeting with everyone that is trying to help. I think you're the tenth person to try this week."

I followed the guard along the cobblestones that lined a path through the courtyard. We came to some stairs and tromped up. My mind began to wander as I followed the guard through the castle. I wasn't sure if I could really do anything. The least I could do was try and maybe make a few coins in the process. Maybe I could make a few coppers and silver from the castle staff. Some of the lords and ladies might be up for music. A gold coin could keep me in comfort for half a year.

But I had confidence that my music could affect people. So others had said. It could be enough. If anything, I knew I had to try. It was my duty as a citizen of the Highlands to help my lord if I could.

The guard led me up a spiral staircase, down a corridor, and into a large bedchamber. An older woman stood at the window, looking out with a lost expression on her face. Her slight form was dressed in a sumptuous green dress, and her brown hair was braided and pinned into place on her head. She turned slowly when we walked through the doorway.

The guard stepped forward and bowed. "The harpist from the village has arrived to try to revive Lord Hamish, my lady."

"Thank you for bringing her to me. You may leave now."

He turned crisply and walked back into the hall.

I looked at the woman, smiling. "I've come to try to play for him."

"Greetings Harpist Mary. I know you play very well. I've heard you play down at the festival in the village. Do you really think it will help?" Her voice was wispy and sad.

I cleared my throat, feeling my nerves try to get the best of me. "People have said I could convince the goddess herself to dance with my talent."

The woman nodded for me to go on. "It is even said that harps are magical instruments. Some even say they can wake anyone, even the dead."

Her ladyship chuckled. "I have heard that saying too." Smiling she continued, "If anything, it will give my heart some cheer. Please." She pointed at a stool near the bed. "Sit near my son."

I bowed again, and moved towards the bed. The curtains draped around it had hidden anyone lying upon it. But when I eased to the side of the bed, I could see a man lying under the covers. His handsome face caught my breath. I watched his chest fall with the rhythm of his breathing. His body looked relaxed, as if his slumber gave him some peace. I sat down determined that I might be able to bring at least some kind of response, if not a complete arousal. He might stir just from listening.

Setting the lap harp upon my knee, I plucked the first chords of a ballad. I let my song glide into a sweet, sensual tone. My eyes closed as I sang. I blended my voice with the chords I plucked. My body moved to the rhythm of the music, and I felt lost as I always did when I performed, lost in another world where hurt and pain could not touch me. When I opened my eyes, his eyes were open and watching me.

My hand went up to my mouth as he said, "Play more for me, beautiful lady."

***

May 8, 1730

I frequently went from the village to the keep to play for Hamish over the next fortnight. He grew in strength from my songs, and was soon eating solid food, drinking water, and sitting up to listen. I delighted in the healing I brought him. I felt a comfortable ease when we were together, just like when we were young. When he looked at me, I felt myself blush to the roots of my hair.

Something started to form in his eyes when we talked. I could not begin to dream what he was thinking. I knew my place. I was only a low-born villager. He was my lord. I possessed no more beauty than any other Highlander lass. But somehow, when he looked at me, I know there was something. His smile was just like it was when we played tag when we were younger, but there was something about the way he looked at me now that was different. Much more different.

I was startled when he asked me to sit beside him. I put my harp on the table, and sat next to him on the bed. I leaned close to him. "What do you need, my lord?"

He whispered, "A kiss."

I smiled at him. "A kiss?" I laughed. "Why such a thing from me?"

"Because you have grown into a beauty, Mary. I always thought so when we were younger." There was a glint in his eyes that reminded me of the trickster youngster he had been. "Did you not wonder why I came so often to play with the other village children? It was because of you."

His smile was a man's now instead of a boy's. I felt a stirring between my legs. He smiled as he continued. "You bring me music to quell the longing in my heart. When you play, the voice stops in my head calling me to join Her in the forest."

He wrapped his arms around me, pulling me closer to him. "You make me want to stay here with you, and not go back to Her."

"I cannot deny you, my lord." I smiled leaning towards him. My heart beat faster. I could not bear to refuse his invitation. He had grown into the most handsome man I'd ever seen. With his wavy brown hair and blue eyes, strapping torso, and muscular arms, he was irresistible.

He pulled me even closer. His lips were warm as they moved over mine. The slightest touch sent shivers through me. I felt his arms wrap around me, securing my body close to him.

I looked up when he stopped. His voice whispered again, "I've come to enjoy your presence, my lady. You feed my soul."

"It is my duty. I must serve you, my lord."

"Call me Hamish. You do more than serve, Mary." He caressed my cheek. "If I had a wish to ask of you?"

I looked into his eyes. "I would happily do what was asked, Hamish."

He breathed in deeply. A longing filled his voice. "Make me forget Her."

Our lips crashed together again. Sensations filled my body as he took control, moving to be on top. Candlelight infused his body with a glow that took on a supernatural quality. His toned chest could be seen through the laces of his shirt.

I felt the cotton of his shirt as my hands caressed his back. He kissed me again, passion driving me to new heights.

My breathing matched his ragged breaths. Each breath and kiss was driving us further. Our bodies were locked in an embrace.

He sat up in mid-kiss, looking down at me. He brushed my red hair as it fanned against the pillows of his bed. "You're my salvation, Mary. The only thing stopping me from going to Her is you."

He kissed me again, moving over the top of my body. His hands caressed the sides of my chemise and bodice. He started to unlace my garments, looking into my eyes as he did so. "All I can think of now is you. I must have you, Mary."

"My lord may take what he needs. I am yours to help you any way I can."

"And your heart?"

I paused for a moment, looking over his face. The rugged jaw was full of tension as it waited for my answer. "My heart is yours, my lord. It's always been yours." I smiled, feeling relieved to finally tell him my true feelings.

He answered me by unlacing my bodice and moving under my chemise to grab my breasts. My back arched as he took each fleshy orb into his mouth, sucking on one nipple and then the other. He teased my nipples, causing me to have shudders through my body. I'd never had a man made me feel this way, wanting him and willing to give him everything.

He stopped to look into my eyes. "I want you to enjoy being with me, my lady. I want to take your heart, not just your body."

"You already do, my lord." I reached for his arms, his chest, caressing down to show how much I enjoyed the sight of him, the smell, the touch. He grabbed at my hand, letting it rest on his chest as I felt down his torso. Then he took my hand and kissed my knuckles and palm. "I promise to give you all the pleasure you give me. These last several days have been my salvation from the curse that has taken over me."

He moved down my body, pulling up my skirts and chemise to feel for my moist slit. I opened my legs wider, inviting him into my secret folds. Hamish felt my slick mound and moved his thumb over my nub to prepare me for him. I squirmed at his touch, moving my legs wider. "Hamish, I want you," I breathed.

My words caused him to grow more against my torso. I could feel his erection ready for me. He eased himself up and began to remove his trews, pulling them off and tossing them to the floor. He eased himself above me, my skirts bellowing on either side. I watched him as he kneeled above me. He took my breath away with his beauty. He pressed his chest against my breasts and whispered, "All this time you've sung for me, you've been the only thing keeping my sanity."

"You're the only thing I want to live for now, my lord."

"Call me Hamish, for I intend to make you my lady." With that, he plunged into me, My cry at his entry spurred him on to pound again and again. I raised my hips to meet him, taking him deep. Each thrust brought us closer to an explosion of passion. I cried for him shouting his name, "My lord Hamish."

He answered, "My sweet Mary." Each thrust into me brought tears to my eyes.

Again and again he pounded. I took him so deep. Our breaths caught as I began to climax. Together, we let go of our passion as the shudders took us both. United in the throes of love magic, I felt my heart join his.

He fell upon me. Breathing slowly, I caressed his face, kissing the top of his nose, cheek, and lips. My voice was breathy when I said, "Hamish, my lord. I love you."

He rose and caressed my head. "As I love you. With all my soul. Nothing will come between us now."

He lay beside me, curling his arms around my waist. I could feel his breathing next to me, lulling me into sleep. I felt safe and loved. The little boy had grown into a man I had fallen in love with. Deep down, I knew I'd always wanted it this way.

Chapter 4

HAMISH

The dreams woke me. I felt a scream echo in the forest near the castle. I felt the tugs on the love bond with the nymph. My heart ripped with pain, and I sat up, gripping my chest. Mary began to stir, and I touched her. It centered me enough to allow me to lay next to her. Touching her broke the spell. I fell back asleep.

In the castle, resting in Mary's arms, I awoke, feeling the pull again. Mary had moved away from me in her sleep. We were not connected. My heart felt like it would stop if I didn't return to the forest. Easing away from my sleeping love, I moved to the floor and picked up my trews. Putting them on, I didn't bother with my boots or cloak. I wouldn't be returning. This time, I'd stay with Her. I didn't look back as I left the bedchamber.

***

I had to go to Her. I could feel Her call to me. I couldn't stop myself. My body longed to be in Her. She was my elixir. I turned for a moment to look down the hall to where my Mary lay. She had made me forget for a while. The call had stopped tugging at my heart for a little while. Mary had made me forget for a moment. For that, I would be forever thankful.

I turned to face towards where I had to go. Through the sleeping castle, I rushed down to the stable yard to get a beast to get me to Her quicker. The horses whinnied in recognition as I entered the stables. I went up to my silver stallion, Wildfire, and let him nuzzle my hand. "Sorry I don't have much for you to eat. But we've got to leave here without attracting much attention." I saddled him and got on his back. "You'll be faster than walking, my friend."

I patted his neck after mounting. Wildfire snorted, familiar with the feel of me on his back. "I know you can come back here on your own. That way they know I made it to where I was going." I guided him through the stable and out into the yard.

I urged him through the open gate, nodding at the guard sitting there. I knew he wouldn't question the business of the heir. He'd let me go without any questions. As soon as I'd gotten the horse sufficiently far away, I broke him into a run. The faster I could get to my beloved nymph, the better. Nothing could stop me now.

***

MARY

I woke with a gasp. I reached next to me and felt nothing but the warmth he had left behind. He was gone, but not too far. I could find him. Something was definitely set upon him. I had to find out what was causing his illness. He had mentioned he was under a curse. That could mean only one thing: magic.

The only thing was to find where he had gone. I dressed and grabbed my harp case. Swinging it on my back, I rushed down through the castle to the stables. I noticed a horse was gone. Biting my lip, I realized he was most likely a goodly distance ahead. I would have to try to track him.

I walked to the open gate. Walking to the guard I asked, "Has Lord Hamish passed this way?"

"Aye. He did." He pointed down the road to the castle. "I watched him gallop down the road heading to the forest not just before sunrise."

I noticed the sun had just peaked over the hills. He could not have left more than half an hour ago. "You've been helpful." I nodded and began the long journey towards the forest. Whatever was causing this illness had to be there. It seemed to be pulling Hamish towards it, and I was going to find out what it was.

HAMISH

Wildfire got me to the glen faster than I could have run. I slid off his back and patted his rump. "Back to the stable, my friend." I hit his backside, and the horse startled. "Get." I hit him again. "Back home." The horse shook its mane and started eating the sweet, green grass that grew around the rocks.

"He doesn't want to leave." I heard Her voice flutter towards me like bells. I turned to see my lover smiling. "I was hoping you'd come back sooner."

I rushed to her, grabbing her into my arms. Holding her close I whispered, "I was ill after our encounter. I've only now recovered."

"It sometimes happens." Clara pouted, and I yearned to make her smile again. "A night with my kind can almost kill a man." She patted my chest. "But you're a strong one. You survived."

"To love you again." I kissed her deeply. I was lost in our embrace, kissing more and faster. I wanted to devour her beauty, to take her again and again on the altar.

She stopped and pushed me back. "Hamish, why did you come back?"

"Because I can't stop thinking about you."

Her smile pierced my heart. "Nor I."

I picked her up and brought her to the stones. Lowering her down, I pulled the gossamer material from her body. It seemed the texture of cobwebs as I removed it from her limbs and flesh. Her perk nipples greeted me as I took to them like a small babe. Her flesh was soft and malleable, smooth to my touch. Her moans followed as my hands caressed her body. I felt down her stomach to her apex of sex.

She whispered, "I'm yours, Hamish. Take me." I leaned over her, brushing her lips with mine.

"No." A woman's voice made me turn. Mary was standing holding her harp. Her face took on a look of determination as she said, "I'm going to free you of the spell, Hamish."

"He's not yours, harpist." My nymph spit the words as she lay beneath my body. She reached up behind my head, pulling me closer. "Take me now, Hamish."

"No. You can't have him. It will kill him this time." Mary struck a chord on the harp, and my nymph flinched underneath me. "My grandmother taught me the song to break the curse of a nymph when I was a child." She looked to me. "I just didn't know what had bespelled you, Hamish." She smiled broadly. "Now that I know…"

Mary began playing a tune. Its chords haunted my heart in its sadness, pulling me towards her. I felt Clara grab me. "Hamish, love me. Take me. Don't listen."

I felt the weight on my chest lessen. I blinked. Looking down, I saw Clara begin to fade. She reached out to me, but I didn't feel the pull like before.

A hissing spilled out of her mouth. "No." I backed away from her, no longer feeling like her prisoner. I could feel my free will returning. The song rose in volume and Clara faded completely away. I eased off the stone slab and moved over to Mary. As I left the circle, I collapsed to the ground. A scream echoed behind me.

Mary stopped playing and ran towards me, holding her harp to the side. "Are you all right Hamish?"

I rubbed my temple. My hands kept me from collapsing fully on the dirt. "I feel dizzy. But I don't feel the pull anymore. The longing is gone."

Except there was one longing that had replaced it. Mary. I looked up at her. "I don't feel drawn here anymore." I stood and caressed her cheek. "I feel drawn to you." Her eyes fluttered as my lips neared hers. I brushed my lips to hers. I grabbed her closer to me and kissed her fully. She returned it, lowering her harp to the ground.

I whispered, "You broke the spell. You saved me."

"I was hoping to."

"You've released me to love now. To love you." I caressed the wood instrument she held. "You both saved me." My hands reached behind her back, pulling her closer. "I want you to stay with me. Come from the village and be my love."

She licked her lips and smiled. "Aye, I will. I think I've always loved you."

I kissed her again, knowing that now fully grown, we could be more than just playmates. I held her feeling what I'd known all those times playing tag. "You were always for me Mary. I know that now too."

I heard her whisper. "Aye. Always."

About The Author

Just when you thought it was safe to go out at night, I arrive on the scene. Greetings darling. I'm **Lynda Belle**. I've always been with you, stalking you when you go to sleep at night. I'm part of your subconscious. I'm the naughty part that wants to come alive with fantasies that would make your mother blush.

I write erotic romances for women that want to forget reality and explore their secret, dirty love. I'm here to take you to those places. I've been hard at work writing adult erotic stories to arouse you to new levels of sensual fantasy. Join me for some dirty love.

For more information on Lynda Belle:

Amazon Author's Page:
https://www.amazon.com/author/lyndabelle

Twitter: https://twitter.com/Lynda_Belle

Website/Blog: http://lyndabelle.com

Newsletter: http://eepul.com/bdhOr5

Acknowledgments

I'd like to thank all of my friends that participate at Renaissance Fairs and Scottish Games through out California. Without you, I wouldn't have the chance to watch amazing men in kilts fighting with two-handed broad swords. Thank you for playing with me.

Lisa and Alain, thanks for being able to take on this project at the last minute. You totally Queen Latifah'ed it. Claudette, thanks for the editing eye you turn onto my manuscripts. You know how to crack all my projects into shape.

To all of you, my readers. You keep me going to pound out story after story. This is all for you.

If you enjoyed this book, please feel free to express your opinion in a review on Amazon or Goodreads. I would appreciate the feedback.

–Lynda Belle

Other hot erotic tales by Lynda Belle:

Scottish Erotic Tales:

Highlander Bride Taken
Highlander Bride Seduction
Highlander Bride Freedom

Hot Groupies Series:

Rockin' Him Hard
Rockin' Him Harder
Rockin' Him Fierce

On Call Series:

The Perfect Escort:
The Perfect Date

Exhibitionists Encounters Series

The Day I Met Her
The Night I Met Him

***All ebooks are Kindle Unlimited titles.

**Soon to be available as omnibus print editions.